Peppa Pig

On the Road

Adapted by Vanessa Moody

SCHOLASTIC INC.

Adapted by Vanessa Moody

All rights reserved. Published by Scholastic Inc., *Publishers since 1920.* SCHOLASTIC and associated logos are trademarks and/or registered trademarks of Scholastic Inc.

ISBN 978-1-338-74098-1

10 9 8 7 6 5 4 3 2 1   21 22 23 24 25
Printed in the U.S.A.   40

First printing 2021

Licensed by

www.peppapig.com
SCHOLASTIC INC.

Peppa and her family live in the United Kingdom. Peppa loves her home, but she has always wanted to visit other places, too.

While making dinner, Peppa spots something shiny. It's a golden ticket! Peppa and her family have won a trip to star in Hash Brown and Super Potato's new movie.

The movie is being filmed in
Hollywood, which is in . . .
"America!" Peppa shouts.

Miss Rabbit flies Peppa and her family all the way across the ocean. They land in New York City.

In New York City, Peppa meets another Miss Rabbit.

"Every town needs a Miss Rabbit!" says the Miss Rabbit from New York. She doesn't sound like the Miss Rabbit that Peppa is used to, though. She has an American accent!

Peppa and her family hop into Miss Rabbit's cab for a tour of New York City.

They see all kinds of things, like really tall buildings.

From the top of the Empire State Building, Peppa uses a telescope.

"Look at me!" says Peppa. She poses with her ice cream, just like the Statue of Liberty!

At night, New York is full of colorful lights.

But looking at a sign for Super Potato makes Peppa
remember. They have to make it to Hollywood for the movie!

Peppa learns that Hollywood is on the other side of America.
She and her family rent a motor home to drive there.

A motor home is like a house on wheels!

It's a long, long drive.

Peppa and her family stop at a diner in the Midwest. It's a place to stretch their legs, use the bathroom, and also . . . to eat!

"Howdy, folks!" says another Miss Rabbit. "Come on in!"

Inside the diner, Peppa and her family eat some fresh eggs made on the grill.

Then Mr. Bob Bobcat and his band play music, and everyone joins in the square dancing—including Mummy and Daddy Pig!

Peppa and George lead a dance.
"Jump up and down like you're in a puddle!" sings Peppa,
while the band plays music.

After the dance, there's a monster truck show! Peppa watches as Mr. Coyote leaps over a big, muddy puddle in his monster truck.

"Wow," Peppa says. She's never seen anything like it.

Daddy Pig can't resist. It's such a great time, he splashes in the mud!

It's good, messy fun.

Peppa loves her visit to the country diner, but it's time to keep traveling to Hollywood.

Peppa and her family are back
on the road.
   "America is a very big country,"
says Mummy Pig.

The desert goes on for miles and miles and miles and miles.

Still, Peppa finds a way to make the road trip fun.
They find treasures along the way—like shells!
A long time ago, the desert was the sea.

As Peppa and her family continue on, they spot Mr. Bison.

"Stop!"
calls Mr. Bison.

Peppa and her family have come upon a canyon.

Peppa learns that the canyon was carved out by a river a long time ago.

A canyon is a deep valley. They come in all shapes and sizes. There are lots of other canyons, too. They call this one the "Grand Canyon."

At the canyon, Peppa meets another Miss Rabbit!

Miss Rabbit sells lots of canyon trinkets. She also sells tours.

Peppa and her family climb into Miss Rabbit's helicopter.

"These rocks have been here since the time of the dinosaurs," Miss Rabbit explains.
"Wow," Peppa says.

The next part of the tour is by boat.
One by one, Peppa and her family climb down a ladder and into a raft.

"Yippee!" squeals Peppa.

The rapids carry the raft safely through the canyon.

When Peppa and her family arrive at the canyon caves, at first, they seem empty.

But Miss Rabbit is there to guide them!
She explains that the people who lived in the caves a long time ago drew pictures on the walls. The drawings tell a story.

A story! That reminds Peppa. Hash Brown and Super Potato's movie!

It's time to keep traveling to Hollywood.

"Are we nearly there yet?" asks
Peppa, back in the motor home.

"You're almost there," says another Miss Rabbit. "Just look for the stars!"

After a long, long, long time, Peppa sees stars on the
ground. She looks up. There's Super Potato and Hash Brown!
She made it to Hollywood.

Super Potato
shows Peppa the
movie studio.
It's time to
make the movie,
*Vegetables in
Space!*

"We look funny in our costumes!"
says Peppa the Broccoli.

Lights! Camera! Action!

It's time for the movie to begin!

Super Potato is filming a battle sequence between himself and some naughty carrots.

But Super Potato doesn't know how to end the movie.

"How will we get rid of all these carrots?" he asks.

Peppa knows just how to save the universe—and the movie!

"We can eat the carrots!" says Peppa.

All the Miss Rabbits are happy to help.

The universe is saved, thanks to Peppa and all the Miss Rabbits!

It's time to go home, but Peppa loved her visit to America.
"The best part was *everything!*" she says.

She can't wait for her next adventure on the road!